Dear Zoe,   4-1-09
  Enjoy a long, happy lifetime
      of learning!
              Donna McNaughton

Learn Along With Lily

by Donna McNaughton

Illustrations by Mike Motz

Raindrop Books • New York

For Ken, Emily and Jenny ~

*with thanks to Musical Moppets for inspiration
and especially to Mike Motz for bringing Lily's world to life.*

~ D.M.

Copyright © 2008 by **Donna McNaughton**
Printed and bound in the United States of America
First printing 2008

Publishers Cataloging-in-Publication Data

McNaughton, Donna.
    Learn along with Lily / by Donna McNaughton ; illustrations by
Mike Motz.
        p. cm.
    Summary: In 13 short poems, Lily Goat learns about colors,
numbers, community helpers, zoo animals, undersea animals,
farm animals, manners, shapes, opposites, the body, family,
transportation, and the rodeo.
    ISBN-13: 978-0-9799677-0-2
    [1. Children's poetry. 2. Learning—Juvenile poetry. 3. Animals—
Juvenile poetry.] I. Motz, Mike, ill. II. Title.

                                    2007937556

To order additional copies please go to:
www.RaindropBooks.com
or email to: donna@raindropbooks.com

Melville, New York
United States

This book was published with the
assistance of the helpful folks at
DragonPencil.
www.DragonPencil.com

Learn Along With Lily

~ Contents ~

Everybody Has a Body

Everybody has a body.
That's how we were made.
In some ways we look different,
but we're pretty much the same.

Lily has two eyes to see,
a cute nose underneath,
two ears to help her listen,
and a smile of clean, white teeth.

She wears a T-shirt on her top;
on bottom, a skirt or pants.
Lily has two arms and legs
and feet so she can dance.

With rings upon her fingers
and nail polish on her toes,
Lily looks so beautiful
everywhere she goes.

Please take care of your body
in everything you do.
You are somebody special,
and I love you!

Lily's Rainbow Day

Lily Goat woke up and said,
"I wish for a **RAINBOW** day."
She put on her **red** sneakers
and went outside to play.

She nibbled a juicy **orange**,
cold and sweet upon her tongue,
and skipped past **yellow** sunflowers
reaching toward the sun.

Lily heard **green** bullfrogs
at the edge of a cool, **blue** pond,
croaking rather noisily,
singing their summer song.

In a field upon the hillside,
Lily stopped to pick
some deep blue **indigo** flowers
and a bunch of **violets**.

Suddenly the rain began, a gentle summer shower—
raindrops dancing everywhere, sprinkling the flowers.

When the sun came out again,
what a nice surprise!
Lily saw a brilliant rainbow
stretched across the sky.

Lily felt so happy
as she skipped along the way.
"Today was simply great.
My wish came true for a **RAINBOW** day!"

7

Community Helpers

Did you ever stop and wonder what makes your neighborhood run?
There are many community helpers and so much to be done.

Our Police and Firefighters are strong and very brave.
They're out there to protect us
and keep our families safe.

OFFICER TROTTA

JOHNNY PUMP

MEDIC AL

If you should need a hospital,
Paramedics will take you there.
Doctors, Nurses, and Dentists work
to give us gentle care.

DR. BYRD

CAREN

DR. FILL

WALKER

HURRIET

MR. KNIGHT

CORA

DEMPSEY

The Bus Driver and
the Crossing Guard
get us where we have to go.
Teachers and Librarians tell us
what we need to know.

It's a good thing we have
Garbage Collectors
to take our trash away.
Remember to put the garbage out.
What day is pickup day?

9

If you stop and think about it,
not much could be better
than to have your own Mail Carrier
delivering your letters.

You don't have to be a grown-up
to help in your neighborhood.
Kids can be good helpers, too,
and pitch in as they should.

There are many important workers as you can plainly see.
What kind of community helper would you like to be?

Lily's Family Reunion

Lily is planning a special day for her family, near and far.
Loved ones will come from all around to picnic in her yard.

Mom and Dad will bring veggie burgers. Sister will buy the buns.
Brother can carry the watermelon.
It's going to be such fun!

Grandma and Grandpa
will take the train
to get there from the city.
Aunt Millie will wear a fancy
hat. She likes to look so pretty.

Uncle Moe is in charge of games.
He knows just what to play.
Lily's cousins will be there, too.
What a terrific day!

There's one thing left to think about;
Lily hopes for a sunny day.
If it rains, they'll move it all into the barn
and have fun anyway!

13

Mind Your Manners

When Lily Goat was younger, her Mom would always say,
"Mind your manners, Lily. Please be polite today."

Be sure to use the magic words:
"Thank you," "You're welcome," and "Please."
It's nice to answer, "Bless you!"
when you hear somebody sneeze.

"Excuse me, may I interrupt?" are just the proper words,
when someone else is speaking and you'd like to be heard.

If you hurt a person's feelings,
there are special words to say:
"I'm sorry—please forgive me"
will help make things okay.

Always mind your manners,
like Lily tries to do.
Show respect for others, and
they'll show respect for you.

You Can Count on Lily

What can you do
if you want to have fun?
Come play with Lily Goat—
Lily's the **one**.

She's never **too** busy
to sing or **to** play.
Try **Tuesday** at **two** o'clock
or even **today**.

If she had **three** wishes,
Lily would say,
"I wish I could eat cupcakes
three times a day!"

Lily likes the **four** seasons—
Spring, Summer, Winter, and Fall—
for each time is special.
She looks **forward** to them all.

16

She uses her **five** senses—
Taste, Touch, Hearing, Smell, and Sight—
to learn about this great big world
from morning
until night.

You can count
on Lily Goat
to help make counting fun.
Let's count backwards with her now:

5, 4, 3, 2, 1!

Down on Whippletree Farm

"Cockadoodle Doo! Wake up—the day is new."
That's how Rooster's day begins
down on Whippletree Farm.

One by one the animals wake.
Listen to the sounds they make,
getting ready for their day
down on Whippletree Farm.

"Oink," grunts Pig. "Good morning."
"Moo," the Cow reports.
Lamb says, "Baa."
"Quack," goes Duck.
Pony stomps and snorts.

Hound Dog lifts his droopy eyes.
Off scoots Red-Tailed Fox.
Spider spins a silky web,
and Goat climbs on the rocks.

Squirrel hides an acorn
as Chicken scratches around.
Rabbit eats a carrot;
Turkey makes a gobble sound.

Goose honks loud
and scares the Cat,
who jumps up on a log.
Hawk soars high
above them all, and
"Ribbit!" goes the Frog.

Who knows what the day will bring?
But as Songbirds start to sing,
the barnyard greets a new morning
down on Whippletree Farm.

19

Do You Know Your Opposites?

The sun comes **up** each **morning** and goes **down** every **night**. The world is always turning— but is it **left** or **right**?

When a traffic light turns red, should you **stop** or **go**? At what speed does a race car travel? **Fast** or **slow**?

Whether you are **short** or **tall**
from your **head** to **toe**,
you can stretch by **reaching high**
or **bending** way down **low**.

IN
OR
OUT?

A door can lead you **in** or **out**
wherever you might be.
You can travel **near** or **far**,
over land or **under sea**.

Answers may be **right** or **wrong**. **Questions** help us grow.
Do you know your opposites? **Yes** or **No**?

How Many Shapes?

Try to imagine
a shape with three sides.
A **triangle** looks like
a nice piece of pie.

With no corners at all,
a **circle** is round.
It looks the same
right-side-up or
upside-down.

One shape has four corners—
square is its name.
All four sides are equal.
(That means they're the same.)

A **rectangle** has corners,
and they number four;
but two of its sides
are stretched out a bit more.

Stop! Look and listen.
You should know this shape.
Let's count all the sides.
An **octagon** has eight.

We see shapes like these
wherever we go.
How many shapes are there?
Does anyone know?

Lily's Undersea Adventure

Lily Goat went to the shore
to visit someplace new.
She built a castle in the sand
and swam the ocean blue.

She dreamed what it would be like
to live beneath the sea
and swim with all its creatures.
How exciting that would be!

She could play along with Dolphin,
watch Whale spout water high,
and wave to Shark and Octopus
as they go gliding by.

She'd ask Oyster for a shiny pearl
(if it wasn't too much trouble).
Then Lily would race Seahorse
and leave a trail of bubbles.

Next she'd ride on Turtle's back
past jiggly Jellyfish,
walk sideways with Crab,
and on Sea Star make a wish.

ZZZ

When Lily's dream was over, she was sad it had to end;
but Lily will remember all her special ocean friends.

Which Way to Go?

There are many ways to get around
in the air, the sea, and on the ground.
Some use engines, steel, and chains,
like **motorcycles**, **cars**, and **trains**.

Ride your **bicycle** over a bridge where a **boat** is sailing by.
Then take a look above you—there's an **airplane** in the sky!

Scooters, **skates**, and **skateboards**
all have wheels that spin around.
Wheelchairs and **strollers** help us out;
they carry us all over town.

A **bus** can help you travel
down a long and busy street;
but if you are not traveling far,
why not use your **feet**?

27

Lily's Rodeo

Everyone's invited!
Come on—it's time to go.
We're headed to the Wild, Wild West
and Lily's Rodeo.

Don't wear a fancy party dress
or pack a three-piece suit.
Make sure you bring a cowboy hat,
some blue jeans, and your boots.

See cowboys ride the broncos
and rope a running calf.
Lily likes the funny clowns—
they always make her laugh.

Lily can play her old guitar and sing some Western tunes:
"Get along little doggies ... Happy trails to you!"

Let's ride ponies down the dusty trail to camp out for the night
and sleep beneath a billion stars beside the campfire light.

Feeding Time at the Zoo

Zookeeper Irwin called Lily Goat.
He said, "I need your help.
It's feeding time at the zoo,
and I can't do it by myself."

Lion and Tiger are wild cats
that eat a lot of meat.
Elephant loves peanuts,
her all-time favorite treat.

City

Give him ripe bananas,
and Monkey will do tricks.
Bear is happy nibbling
wild berries on a stick.

Snake and Alligator
eat their food in one big bite.
Peacock and Ostrich think
wiggly worms taste just right.

DO NOT
FEED THE
ANIMALS

Zoo

It's lots of leafy vegetables for Hippo and Giraffe.

A black and white cookie
is Zebra's dessert.
(She likes the chocolate half!)

After Lily and Irwin finish
feeding the animals at the zoo,
the two of them sit down
for a delicious dinner, too!